# 6 - 6 - 0

Michael Munro

Blue Swell Books
Nanaimo, B.C.
Canada

First Print Edition: January 2016
ISBN: 978-1-988257-00-6

## Acknowledgements

This is a work of art, probably, maybe. All of what you read is mostly true only the names have been changed to protect the innocent. But let's face it, none of them are innocent so I used the names that I called them when living or around. If I've offended anyone, that's my job and not an intention, or maybe it was.

Thank you to my smoking hot wife and wonderful children who make me laugh no matter what.

To the mother of that guy I worked with who I told on the phone while working at Colour Your World that he was running up and down the aisles screaming "I am the Ayatollah Khomeini" with a white towel wrapped around his head... I'm not sorry. That was funny. And I don't care that I was fired.

And especially thanks to the drummer of Aqua. Without you baby there would be no rhythm and no music.

## The Hole

The sun poured over the Cascade
Mountains and fell towards the unemployment
ripped ocean side coal town. Hydro worker
Bert Johnson sensed the bit grinding itself to
pieces six or seven feet below his boots. The
brand new 1956 Chevy 454 revved into high
gear within the heavy duty flatbed truck as his
buddy and co-worker David Johnston (no
relation) gunned the engine to provide the
pickup running the drill bit with more power.

"What the fuck is it Bertie? Can you
see?" He wiped the sweat from his brow.

Bert leaned over the hole as best he
could and yelled back a "dunno" along with a
shrug. They'd been drilling the new power
poles for weeks into the Seven Acres farmland
that was seeing massive development. The old
seven acre farms were being sold and turned
into miner's huts and bank executive two-
storey 1600 sq. ft. mansions left and right as

developers bought cheap land in a cheap town and built cheap houses.

"She's definitely grinding. It's got to be that fucking bedrock again. She goes straight down to hell I bet."

"Back it off Davey. I think we're just grinding metal here."

The 454 whine eased off and the bit slowed down to allow the two men to yell without shouting at each other.

"Richard's gonna be pissed if we blow another engine, eh?"

Both Bert and Davey chuckled and wiped more sweat from their brows.

"I think we'd better pull her out and gauge the depth on it. I bet we've got enough now anyways. We'll take lunch and move onto the next one. I figure we can get four more done today," Davey yelled at Bert.

"Yeah I think so," Bert said, taking a step towards the bit.

"Ease her up real slow now Davey. Hey, did you bring any of that Crown Royal? I sure as hell need a pull on that. Did you watch the Tommy Hunter show last night?"

"Yeah. God awful show. I've got some Crown for lunch, you bet," said Davey as he grabbed the levers and pulled down on the shifter at the side of the flatbed and began lifting the 20" wide auger. As he did he reversed it and dirt started to slowly spray off the bit and around the hole.

In a second they could both hear metal grinding on rock and the auger began to slow down and stop.

"Damn it all to hell. This ain't gonna be easy."

Davey reversed the auger and it moved a little. Then he reversed it again trying to throw the rock off.

As he did Bert leaned in towards the auger with his giant 14-foot pry bar to see if he could untangle it. As he moved the ground underneath his left foot collapsed and he fell forward toward the bit automatically moving his right hand up and catching it.

Davey felt the auger bite his friend as he saw it. So quickly his yell was more of a reaction from his throat than an actual word. Bert spun into the drill bit and down the hole his head snapping back as it went down the two or three inches before his neck, arms splaying upwards and following the torso and feet spinning once, twice and down. In an instant the auger came loose and spun blood at first then pieces of Bert in a splattering radius hitting the truck and Davey.

By the time Bert came up Davey had panicked pushing the speed lever higher as he moved his hand from it and then he had run forward to grab Bert and fell forward in the soft dirt and quickly spun around the bloody bit following Bert into the hole.

From the fields beside the truck cows chewed their grass as the engine remained gunned and the bit spun blood, then dirt, then nothing until the fuel tank ran dry which at full throttle would be later that evening if the engine didn't seize first.

Back at the hydro office Davey and Bert's colleagues were cleaning their mud off their shoes and changing into civilian clothes. There was always a brief smoke in the main room as time cards were punched and tomorrow's plans were hashed out. Single light fixtures dotted the large space and pierced through the blue cigarette smoke. Tattered wallpaper and dark lacquered wood paneling finished the motif. The room echoed with the din of men and their finished days.

Damian Howard, crew boss, counted the cards and tallied the holes and prepared the plans for next week. Within minutes it was noticed that Bert and Dave's stalls were still and silent.

"Hey Howard!" one of them shouted.

Howard looked up from his pencil and large construction desk while he nursed the last bit of tobacco from his heater.

"Meh?" he replied and went back to his cutblocks.

"Bert and Davey get approved for overtime? 'Cause you know, I could use a little extra work myself. You know Sandra's pregnant."

"Fuck, wasn't me," replied Howard without missing a beat.

A loud roar of laughter echoed around the room.

"No, shit no, there's no overtime this month. You know we're over budget. How late are they?"

Howard looked up at the clock.

"Is their truck in the lot?" BC Hydro's new truck was $4,000 of government purchase and Howard was starting to worry that those two twits had dumped it in the ditch. Howard had been with Bert and Dave in the Royal Patricia's and spent a lot of time at Gold Beach together and then France, Holland and Germany. They had shared blood, sweat and bullets together. They were twits but they were never late.

Howard grabbed yesterday's work docket and ripped through the sheets until he found them. A silence began falling in the large room. It was a fact of the job. An unspoken danger that they all understood. No one was laughing now.

"Can I get a couple of volunteers to run out to Seven Acres please? I'll authorize some overtime. Take a truck and some chain in case they've dumped it in a ditch." Howard chewed his cigarette and dumped ashes all over himself and the desk and paperwork.

"Yeah I got it boss. I need the OT."

"Me too, I'm in."

Howard looked up.

"All right you guys. I'll stay here. We'll work radios on channel 4. Got about 3 hours daylight left. You can't miss it. Go straight off Victoria Road and head north. It's a bit rough but should be fine."

"You got it boss."

The two saddled up and the door opened and closed. In a few minutes an engine jumped to life. The rest of the men quietly grabbed their gear and headed home all hoping for the best.

Howard found their files in case spouses had to be notified.

The old pick up truck had a suspension like a tank and the two riders were jarred on every bump, their asses feeling every rock as it swayed back and forth on the gravel road.

Within half an hour they came upon Bert and Davey's brand new truck. Howard's pets they called them. They always got the best gear, best helmets.

"What the fuck?"

They could hear the truck was running at full and there was no one around.

They parked the truck and got out wondering if maybe they had a bear encounter and fucked off across the field. Maybe a cougar. It would take a lot to get old Bert and Davey to shit their pants though.

When they came around the side of the truck one of them grabbed the lever and throttled the engine back and slowed the bit down and finally off. It was still spinning but not making a sound. Must have sheared the tip off. Bert and Davey were damned lucky the engine hadn't seized.

When the man who had turned off the lever wiped the sweat from his face he looked at the bit and could see what seemed to be red mud everywhere.

That's when he noticed his friend screaming at him.

"You're covered in it! Oh my fucking God. It's all over you man."

He looked at his hand and noticed it was covered in red. And then he noticed the two helmets on the ground and the pieces of human body and boots with feet up to the ankle still in them.

Then he vomited.

One of them radioed in.

"Jesus, oh Jesus."

Two weeks later Damian Howard ordered the procession forward in Seven Acres.

"Not that hole."

"Look," Howard said not glancing up from his paperwork and smoke, "We have to proceed. I miss Dave and Bert too. But I need that pole planted and we have one week to finish that subdivision. We're stringing wires in August and I have a boss too. It sucks but we can't stop here."

"But Jesus. The same fucking hole?"

"That whole area is bed rocked. You know that. We're down seven feet. Lop a foot off the pole, guide wire it tight and move on for fuck sakes," Howard said, then looked up.

He watched them leave the hall and close the door and heard the trucks fire up to life. He pulled his desk drawer open and pulled out a bottle of scotch and a glass and poured a large one. Under the bottle he took out a fading picture of him with Bert and Dave in Holland standing in a field surrounded by Nazi SS dead soldiers. Bertie had his foot on one of their asses.

He blinked back a tear.

"Damn it."

# Chapter 1

Harewood was a Canadian ghetto if that existed. The Indian reserve perpetuated a constant flow of drug addicts and alcoholics. The Hells Angels owned the city council and made sure that this particular area of the city contained all the crack heads and low lifes while the rest of the northern part of the city contained those that worked for the city. They only ventured to the south part to buy their addictions. A piece of rock, ass, grass – a virtual candy store of sin.

Some of the less fortunate young families, hard working though they may have been, could never have afforded the northern part and so were stuck buying homes in the ghetto and fighting daily with the prostitutes and drug addicts to move along to no avail.

Joe Davidson started off ok. He had a job at the mill. He got a house in Harewood. A bit of a nice piece of ass with an Indian girl who sometimes was sober. He got a boat and a sundeck and two kids. At first he dabbled a bit in the alcohol. He would knock off a case of beer on a weekend. Then it was a case of beer on a Friday night with the boys, one on Saturday for the hockey game and for good measure one on Sunday for the lawn work leaving him showing up for work at the mill on Monday smelling like a brewery.

"You know Joe, you're a really good worker. And everyone here thinks you're our best welder. And the truth is you probably are our best welder."

Joe stared blankly at the man in the tie and shirt behind the desk. Joe was worried about his balding hair and growing paunch but not his job. They needed him. And everyone drank beers. This was just grinding his balls to make his boss look good. Joe knew it. Company policy was to talk to him about drinking if they suspected it. He'd get a few warnings before they did a damn thing about it and besides he could clean up if he wanted to. Everyone thought it was pretty damned funny,

him showing up smelling like Lucky beer.
They were starting to call him Lucky too. Sure,
there was the odd guy that would snicker at
him behind his back. But for the most part not
in front of his face. Joe could easily handle his
own. His boys had learned that. From time-to-
time he had to take them out in the alley and
punch them around a bit to remind them that
he was Lucky Joe. A few times the cops were
called but the blood was cleaned up by the
time the boys arrived. And everyone did it.
You don't knock your teenage boy in the teeth
or you'll get a boy that's ruined. Joe absently
rubbed his face. His own dad saw to his
upbringing. More than once hitting him in the
head with a blank piece of wood until he got
the point for whatever it was he did wrong. He
had learned the right way to do things by God.
And now his sons would learn to. Last night he
had been drinking with his 16 year old Joey
and Joey Jr. had lipped him off and he had
dropped JJ with one punch. He chuckled a bit
as he rubbed his hand.

"And Joe, well, the thing is the wood
supply is running low, as you know. Used to be
first growth timber supply was everywhere.
Now we have to truck it in from way up north.
Costs are getting higher and higher. We're
looking for efficiencies. It's the only way we

can compete in this tough market Joe. Damn, time was pulp was $14/tonne, now, well, God we're lucky if we can $3. It's really collapsed with those fucking twats from Brazil pulling on line. Fact of the matter is I don't know if I will keep my job. Anyways, Joe, what I'm trying to say is that, well, it looks like we have to let you go. I'm sorry. It isn't my call. But you know you're a damned good welder. You need a reference, you call me. I'll make sure it's a layoff (he pulled his fingers back and forth in air quotes beside his head) so that you'll get EI. Good luck Joe."

Joe shook the hand, got in the pick up truck, and started drinking the few beers he had stashed in his truck as he drove home.

Once the beer didn't dull the pain he started smoking the pot his boys brung home. It wasn't half bad. Swore he saw Jesus on more than a few occasions. Sometimes his bitch wife would come into the garage where he did odd jobs for money with his welder and she would bitch at him to sober up and get a job. Sometimes his sons would try and get him to sober up or stop smoking pot and he would beat them in the alley. Finally he started poking around downtown on his walks for booze. After getting a blow job from a hooker in the alley on Victoria Street by the Indian Reserve she offered him some blow. Which he did, and loved. Then he started to sell his tools for the cocaine and crack. Then his boat and hot tub for the crack. And when he couldn't pay anymore the Vietnamese showed up.

"Get in the van Joe."

He looked down at the small little fella holding a knife to his stomach. And then at the four guys waiting in the blue minivan. His first realization that he had fucked up. He hadn't seen his bitch wife in two or maybe three weeks. All of his stuff was gone. And now this. A knife or a ride.

"I'm not getting in there!" he screamed.

Two of them got out with baseball bats and smashed his knee caps. They grabbed his wallet as he lay on the ground and emptied what little cash he had and grabbed his almost maxed Visa card and his welding equipment and loaded it into the van.

"You fucking pay Joe, or we fucking kill you. Understand?"

A steel toed boat lifted his face from the mud and he peered up at a bland face with long black hair and steel black eyes.

"You don't fuck with us, got it?"

"Yeah, I got it."

Then they were gone but the limp stayed with Joe.

And so he limped around his house making garbage filled dinner and wondering where that bitch was. When his sons showed up he would do hits of crack with them and maybe some pot. When his welfare cheque showed he would drain it on scotch and some food from the 7-11.

It must have been around midnight when the door opened a crack and he saw a familiar face peer into the shit stained bedroom.

"Hi Joe."

It was bitch face. 'Til death do us part. Well… she had left early.

"Where you been, you fucking skank," he stammered out. His head hurt like hell and his eyes were bloodshot past returning to white at some point in the next year.

"I've come for my stuff. My God, Joe, what have you done? You've got to start taking care of yourself. Did you sign the divorce papers that my lawyer mailed? I'm getting married next month."

"What?"

"Yeah, I'm moving in with him tomorrow. I've got a truck in the alley for my stuff Joe. I'm sorry it didn't work out with you but you know…" she shrugged and looked around at the beer cans and bottles of scotch and rum and vodka and used needles and burned spoons.

"This ain't no good anymore Joe."

Bitch was right.

Damn it.

"Yeah," he mumbled as he ran his hand through his bald head.

"Yeah I got it sweetie," he said standing up.

Together they started loading her van.

Joe realized it was over. Life, marriage, job. All gone.

Except a half finished bottle of rum in the torn apart kitchen from some wild party at some point in the past.

He grabbed at the neck and began drinking.

Then he drained it.

Feeling warmer he hoped he could patch it up with bitch face.

She wasn't a bad little piece of ass as far as those go. A nice tight package with hard little titties.

"Baby..." he slurred at her.

There must have been a tear in his eye because she hugged him.

He grabbed her hair and punched her in the face landing a beauty in the nose.

As she squealed he dropped her to the ground amongst the garbage and pulled her tight jeans off and finally her underwear and pulled out his cock and spread her legs becoming harder by the second as she struggled below him.

He grunted as he entered her and started to get to work.

"No!" was all she would say. Quieter now.

Finally when he was finished she pulled up her panties and ran out.

Realizing it might have been rape and a bad thing Joe pulled up his underwear and chased the bitch and drops of blood after her into the pouring rain.

He caught her under the streetlight by her long flowing black hair.

The neighbours briefly opened their windows when she was screaming but they had seen Joe before and the police came and had never done anything anyways and they still had Joe living beside them knowing the police could do sweet fuck all so they closed their window and draped their lights and he went to work on her under the streetlight.

First knocking out all her front teeth. Then he kneed her in the face partially removing her nose and ripping apart skin above her eye which dangled above the eye closing it.

The streetlight began to flicker and go out.

The streetlight that bathed his house in light for so many years finally began to flicker and fade. Harewood, Seven Acres. There used to be fields of cows here. Now there was just a bunch of old miner's huts and gravel lanes and fading lives.

As the light flickered, dimmed and went out Joe thought he felt or saw a red shape near him. Over his shoulder. Felt a hand on his shoulder patting him on the back as he put his hands around her neck and began to squeeze. A laughter, his or someone else's rang in his ears. He could feel the bones snap under his strength and her eyes bulge and dim and the blood drain from her mouth and nose and drip down with the rain onto his feet.

"More," he felt or heard. Again that redness that feeling of heat that he sometimes got with the crack cocaine. The rush of the heroin when he juiced. Bitch face seemed to be pitched at an odd angle.

"More," he heard in the darkness.

As he ripped her panties off and stroked himself to erection he felt heat on his backside.

More as he dumped his cock into her dead body.

"Mmmmm," he mumbled as he started to pump her.

Bitch face was getting what she deserved.

Then the blue and red lights started to enter his peripheral vision, then he could clearly see them on his house, on his neighbours.

Just as he was coming the light flickered back on.

The police would only say it was the most gruesome thing they had ever witnessed. One of the guys in the squad car had to take six months of therapy and several more of hard drinking to put the vision behind him.

Joe's bare ass moving up and down on his dead wife's saddle while her head was tucked under her body.

They had beaten Joe with their night sticks for at least 20 minutes before finally dumping him in the back of the car and throwing up behind it.

## Chapter 2

Janis Hartlyn was a slut. She then became a prostitute. It was a natural progression. Eventually she had fucked almost everyone in town that was interested. She enjoyed the physical pleasure of touch more than the verbal appreciation of communication. If you got Janis drunk you could usually get her underneath you without too much coercion. Eventually she met Bubba. Now Bubba could fuck. She liked his hard cock and the way he caressed her ass during sex. He was also mean as hell and she liked the power that came from being around Bubba who had dabbled in prison. A few stabbing stints. A couple of minor rapes. A couple of small bank robberies. His piercing blue eyes were usually all it took to get what he wanted. No one ever doubted big Bubba. He was the King of Harewood. Bubba made his money off women. He would fuck girls like Janis, then dump a needle in her arm, inject her with crack and have himself a loyal worker as long as she was strung out. Bubba made frequent deals with his friends at Hells Angels to keep enough heroin around to satisfy his workers. Occasionally he would get some asshole from the north end making a small purchase. Sometimes the Angels would ask him to do some collecting in the north end to make a little extra cash. He was on one of those runs now. He had the little prick by the throat. Bubba may have bought and sold drugs, hit women, injected women, stolen from banks, stabbed a few people, but Bubba never, ever stole from other people, just banks. He hated this little punk ass for being a thief. Sitting there all high and mighty in his north end house with his fancy carpet and fancy roof and fancy living room tv and fancy table. He shit on the carpet and smashed the tv when he first walked in to let his presence be known. Everyone knew Bubba. And now this little punk ass knew.

"You owe."

"I know, I know, I know," he squawked. His little grey eyes were starting to water from his grip around his neck. He heard and smelled the piss running down the man's leg. Bubba always kept them at arms length knowing they would piss and shit themselves. Sometimes he wore rubber boots when he remembered. But this time he had forgotten to change. He looked at the clock on the stove. Almost 8:30pm. Time for the punch, the promise and to get back to his hos and make sure they were working. Business was good and he was damned if he was going to let his foot off the accelerator this time. Not when he was nearing in on his nestegg. His goal was to start his own gang. Get down to Mexico and make his connections and start importing himself and bypass the Angels all together. Fuck, if they needed him so much to do their dirty work, then he might as well just fucking do the whole damned thing himself. There's no point in this small change shit anymore. The fuck business was okay but it never got better, never got worse. It was what it was. A few thousand a month, a few thousand a month more for collections. A couple thousand here and there with robberies. But that's all there was in this small shit hole. The real money was at the top where the importing was. That's where he intended to be.

He punched the puke in the stomach.

"You pay or I'm back and I'll fuck your wife."

He pulled out his enormous cock.

"With this."

He slapped it on the man's head who had fallen onto the carpet.

Then he grabbed his balls.

"You and I know that she's going to like it too."

Then the ritual zip up, the pant pull up, the leg pull back, and the boot to the stomach. Never the face. A man had work to do if he was going to pay his debt. He never kicked too hard in case it caused internal bleeding and a stop at the hospital where questions were asked and again, no money, just a dead body later on when the punk ass didn't pay, and then he had questions to answer. That usually involved having a molar pulled with pliers'. That was never fun. So he was careful to leave him in agony mentally and physically, but able to mortgage the mortgage and lien the car or do whatever the fuck it took to come up with the $10,000 they usually owed. No one called Bubba for less than 5K. Bubba wasn't cheap.

The King of Harewood returned to his red piece of shit Lincoln with the torn drop top, black, with white pieces of it flying back in the wind. Bubba lit a cigarette and snorted some coke. Then when he was proper flying he turned on the Lincoln and eased on to Departure Bay Road and nursed the piece of shit back to Harewood in the fading light.

When Bubba got back he was tripping. He parked the car somewhat gently into the bumper of the car that was stopped in front of what he was pretty sure was his place on Colliery. He was pretty sure Hydro had finally cut off this piece of shit. Fucking Joe was a dumb motherfucker that never paid his bills. Crack head. Always buying booze or crack. Bubba never touched the stuff. He had heard about Joe fucking his wife under the streetlight when her neck was snapped a couple of months ago. Fuck, Bubba was living in the basement. Bubba lived where Bubba wanted. Usually with stupid mother fuckers who owed the Angels. And Joe most certainly did. Fact was if Joe hadn't been nailed for murder Bubba was going to strap him to a chair and dump 240 volts through his dumbass anyways. Joe's debt was through the roof. And so were his friends. All of them always thought Bubba was their friend too until he turned those blue eyes on them. Then they realized that they weren't friends at all. A couple of months ago one of Joe's friends had failed to pay their debt. Bubba held him down while another collector cut off his finger. The neighbours or some shit called the police. The guy was still bleeding all over himself and the alley when the police showed up. No one said nothing. Bubba laughed a little.

No power, no problem. He'd send that little slut Janis to the store for some smokes, count his money, maybe snort a little.

What Janis liked about Bubba is when he stopped hitting her sometimes he was real nice to her. Sometimes he fucked her real slow and gentle too like he loved her. She was pretty sure he did. He always came so hard on her. She knew it wasn't fake. She knew Bubba was planning on something. She was pretty sure he was going to make sure he took her with him, wherever that was. For now she took the punches to the face from time to time from Bubba when he wanted to make sure she was giving him half her money for protection. Bubba was pretty handy she had to admit. If a John knew that Bubba was her boy they didn't hurt her. And they paid, usually before hand, before she got down on her knees and blew them.

When she came home on this night it was raining. The grass was grown over. Bubba and his friend had been staying at this Joe's place and his mom's place. His mom didn't live there she only owned the place. She owned both places Joe said, between blow jobs. Joe always talked a lot between his fucking. She would be first to Joe on welfare day to make sure she got her $50 and always, always, gave her $25 to Bubba. Joe made sure Bubba knew always telling him, I paid her $50 Bubba, she's ok, you don't have to hit her. Bubba would grunt or laugh or hug little Janis and rub her hair.

"Awe, this little sweet thing. No way. She's my little money maker." And then he would laugh and pat her ass.

Janis knew he loved her. He never really really hurt her. She had been on collection once and seen Bubba run into another pimp, the Apple Pimp. He was a big big man and she was worried her Bubba had met his match. But Bubba dropped the Apple Pimp with one punch. His knees buckling. Then he had pulled out his big pecker and dropped it on the man's head and asked her to take a picture with her old camera phone. She liked that photo when the camera was charged. When she remember to charge it. When she remembered where it was.

She came home and pulled her wet jacket off. That's when the hand flashed into her face and the stars or round circles and blackness and brownness closed in on her and she felt the pain and her knees buckled and she fell to the ground in the darkness and the tears started and she dropped her bags of stuff from the 7-11. Bubba was high. She just knew it. He was shifting from one foot to the other. She hated that. Hated not knowing which foot was going to kick her. She grabbed the right one through the tears and head ringing and almost pitch blackness. Just a little light shone through the kitchen window of the dingy 70's dated kitchen with its yellowed linoleum floor that was missing pieces and the cupboards that were missing doors and handles and hanging crooked from one too many benders.

She spat blood onto the boot.

"Please no baby. I've been good, I promise."

Bubba looked down on her. There really was no reason to have hit her. He just felt like it. Sometimes Bubba had this mean streak that would come out and he couldn't control it. Sometimes he just got this snicker, or felt this snicker, come across his face and he thought to himself, not really thinking, it was just a flash of a thought – what would it be like to punch her in the face – then he just did it.

The result was somewhat satisfying. She had dropped like a sack of shit and was spitting blood on his runners. She was wet and crying and he was wet and high and hungry. He grabbed the bags of shit from 7-11 and opened them up and found a bit of chips and pop and some candy bars and a banana? What the fuck? He hadn't had one in so long. So he ate that. There was a piece of meat too. So he went downstairs and started up the barbecue that he had brought in to use for heat, light and cooking. This was always a necessity when the banks started the foreclosure action. Bubba usually lived rent free in the homes of junkies that were being foreclosed. It was cheap and he was always the biggest in the house so he took the room that he most fancied and lived rent free. Sometimes they shut off the water and that was a bitch but he would just send his women to go and get bottled water and they usually got another 90 days. Sometimes the house was owned by the Hells Angels and they wanted it burned down for insurance purposes. So they would demo it, then fuck the city over for some free water and sewage and hydro for some free power and cable as long as they could and then burn the mother fucker down the day before the sheriff showed up with his big pompity ass wagon and his stupid letters of eviction that he would stamp up on the door. Usually Bubba would take one and take a shit on it and leave it on the floor just inside the front door as a calling card IF they weren't burning it down. Then he wouldn't waste his time. He would just start the barbecue gas up, not light, let it linger till he could smell the fumes upstairs when it was downstairs. He would sit in the house for as long as he could, then quickly he would open and close the door and leave and go to the downstairs window, smash it, flick a match in and run down the alley or street while the house blew up and the insurance agents wept in their pants. That's how the Angels had managed to secure about a quarter of the town. They made a profit coming or going. Burning or paying. The Angels took profit.

Once he had fed he found Janis on the floor and picked her up and hugged her and stroked her ass and told her he was sorry that he was a bit high on cocaine and he would never do that again and then he asked her if she had made any money, did she have any problems that she needed sorting out. He kissed her gently and dried her face with his shirt sleeve and gave her the rest of the food in the bag.

Janis loved this part. She loved this part of the making up when he would take her to the bedroom and ride her. Sometimes her cunt hurt a little bit. Sometimes a lot depending on when she'd seen the doctor last. But mostly it was good. He was a beast in bed. She ate what she was given in the darkness and listened to the wind blow and the rain patter against the roof glad to have Bubba near for protection. The light flickered for a second from the streetlight outside. She listened to the rain some more and thought about her last customer and how he had insisted on cumming on her face and how she had said that was $30 extra. She told Bubba. For some strange reason Bubba got this weird look on his face and jabbed her with a needle and that's when she blacked out.

Jason looked out his bedroom window at that crack house at exactly the same time as Bubba was dragging this half dressed woman across the alley and then the backyard and into the house that Joe's mom owned. All by her hair. All while she was kicking and screaming. Jason woke up his wife. "Oh my God. Did you see that?"

"What dear?"

"This guy just pulled a woman by her hair out of Joe's place and across to his mother's place."

"Close the blinds. There's nothing we can do for her. They'll know it was us that called now just close the damned blinds."

He did.

Janis was in a basement with one of Bubba's friends. Both had their dicks out. Both were taking turns fucking her while she was tied to the bed. She plead for her life between fucks.

Bubba and that guy were drinking from the bottle. And then they took that bottle sometimes and put it in her until she screamed. Then she was fucked some more. Sometimes they took their cigarettes and butted them out on her stomach or thighs. It seemed to go on for hours until they passed out. She had managed to rub her hands through the straps that were holding her and she grabbed her clothes and dressed and quietly opened the front door and ran to the neighbour's house.

She was greeted by a woman in her thirties who let her in. She sat in a chair and exploded her ordeal until the police were called and she left in the cop car.

They found him on the Island Highway in his piece of shit Lincoln heading north. At about 70 in a 90 zone. High on cocaine and booze and with her blood all over his shoes and his shirt.

"Who the fuck was the other guy you piece of crap?" the cop asked.

The video of the interrogation clearly has him saying, "What other guy? Who are you talking about? It was just me and Janis and it was consensual."

"You broke a bottle off inside her you scum bag."

It clearly showed the cop wanting to hit big Bubba but his partner grabbing his hand and pulling it down. And then that cop hit him.

## Chapter 3

Naturally Joe's teenage boys got into drugs. They sold it to their dad to make money. Just because he was in jail didn't mean they stopped sales. In fact, because they got sympathy, business was good. So good that the youngest one, Joey, got himself a brand new 10 year old white Honda Prelude with tail wing and ground effects and 200 W stereo. Joey and his brother at times drove together. At times they competed for the same dollar. And then friction would get the better of them and then Joey and Keith would butt heads much to the delight of the pack of boys that wanted danger but not too much. Just a little bad boy was good for the image, good to get pussy. A little too much and then it was all bad. So they rode with Joey. And Keith mainly drove alone in his early '90s green Ford Aerostar minivan. A pretty good cover in fact as no one expected a family man to be selling drugs. And it had lots of room in the back for whatever the customer needed – help shooting up, a blow job from his wife, whatever. Keith had two kids and was pretty sure they were his. He'd spent about three of the seven years after his class graduated from high school in jail. His dad would sometimes drop in with a bag of beef and a carton of smokes at Brannen Lake Penitentiary. If was he at William Head, a medium security, then it was too far for dear old dad to stay sober. That was hard time. Because his little shit brother Joey was too busy scooping his customers and too busy fucking that fat broad Helen with the skin tight white shirts and the black bras that popped her nipples out to come and see him. Those William Head days had turned Keith in to a bitter person. Not that he was generally optimistic in life anyways. It was a hard thing for him to accept when he was kicked out of the house by his dad Joe after Keith had beat him badly in the alley. It was hard when you realized you were twice as strong as the old man and there was nothing left at the house for you but a bag of bad memories and a mom that was gone somewhere in Vancouver doing God knows what to make money. From time to time she would sober up and bust him a phone call.

"Keith, baby… Do you have any money?"

"Yeah mom. How much do you need?"

So the family depended on Keith.

Keith to take care of his mom and dad and to watch out for little Joey who was their baby darling and who Keith had to admit quite possibly could still have a chance at life. All of these things rolled through Keith's head as he sat in the van coming back from Brannen Lake lock up for the past 30 days for a DUI, driving without insurance, driving without due care, driving without a license, driving while prohibited and violating his parole. The rest the judge could give a damn about. It was that last one that he looked down upon Keith and sighed and smacked the gavel and gave him six months in the hole. With good behaviour Keith was out in 30.

Keith was a good inmate. Popular with the guards and the inmates. He was quick to start a card game. Good with a joke. Time went fairly easy for him at Brannen and the boys were always glad to see him back.

Johnny Hollywood on the other hand, was quite simply, fucked. His face was all over

American television, America's Most Wanted.
That prick. So he had killed a few people, big
whoop. Johnny was a cool little package of
American heat. Shaved head. Always dressed
in white t-shirts, clean, clean jeans, clean shoes,
clean teeth. A drug dealer but no ordinary
dealer. He never touched the shit. Never. No
exceptions. No drinking, no drugs. Didn't need
it. When a friend of his owed him $50 for a
drug debt, no worries. Johnny Hollywood
grabbed that .38 and found that little cockroach
just off the strip in LA and he punched him
hard in the stomach and threw him in the back
of the car and drove to the beach and put that
shiny black gun under his chin and squeezed
the trigger. Not even a drip of blood on his
shirt. He packed his shit and headed north.
Crossed the border at Blaine got into
Vancouver and into the Marble Arch pussy
parade faster than you can say one day. He was
smooth. Never a bead of sweat graced his
forehead. By the time he hit Oregon State that
murder was long long gone from Johnny's
brain. He had the future in mind. Running,
sure, but the future. A new start in Can A Duh.
A nice wife, a nice house, a new car. He gave
himself one year. And so Johnny Hollywood
sat sipping his beer at the Marble Arch in the
din and the big titted starlets swirled around

and the bartender chewed his toothpick and watched for trouble and from time to time had to remove the odd drunk who got a little too close to the kittens. And slowly Johnny started to make a few inquiries about the darker side of life in Can A Duh. He was no dummy. Johnny Hollywood recognized the university crowd and stayed clear. Johnny knew the working stiff who had married too young and was in looking at what might have been if he had just studied a little harder and a little luck had gone his way. He knew the off duty cop, the undercover fuzz and stayed clear. And of course there was the barflies. The third Wednesday of every month saw a few come in. As it happened he was there on just one of thus such Wednesdays and he was able to buy a beer for this particular barfly and found out some valuable information about where the drugs were, who ran the town, whose bar this was, what cops were seedy which were straight. You can learn a lot in 12 hours sitting beside a barfly if you paid in beer. Johnny had brought a few thousand with him. No one seemed to care about the greenbacks going out and the Canadian buck coming back. Since no one had batted an eye at the first Benjamin or the subsequents Johnny knew this was a bought house. Paid for and run by the organization. His money was good here. His car with the American plates was easy. He waited until 2 am the first night and during a convenient rain storm and wind that came with it he had snapped plates off a Canadian Chrysler mini-van and dropped it on his Honda Civic, grey, plain Jane. Johnny knew never to draw attention to himself. No flash. No dash. Johnny was all business. There was risk of course. Uniformed police might come in and look around at the customers. There were still some that did their jobs. And that was a bathroom break. He always sat closest to the bathroom for that exact reason. So after a couple of days at the bar and a couple of nights in his car that was parked in the back lot of the titty twister something finally happened.

While chewing his bar burger and fries two Asian men sat down at his table. A photograph of his "wanted" face from the American border service and FBI "Most Wanted" list gently flapped to a stop under his face.

Johnny Hollywood, wanted for murder, drug trafficking, extortion, robbery and some other crap looked up at him. He had a cleanly shaven face and head and dark blue eyes, 5'6" and 150 lbs. of childhood gone wrong. A very young Bruce Willis, very handsome, and lethal lying near his French fries. He grabbed the piece of paper and looked back at the black eyes and straight black hair. This was a man who meant what he said. Johnny took note of the lines near his eyes and the lines around his mouth. Long lines from sitting motionless squinting into the sun and waiting on haunches, Johnny guessed. Johnny had seen enough war veterans to know this was one. The eyes that didn't twitch and never moved off of his, eyes that had a stare, a knowing of seeing a lot of death. Eyes that would see him dead here in his seat as if he were a fly being swatted on a window. A lot of death was staring back at him. Maybe he's seen a lot of shit in Cambodia. Maybe it was Vietnam. Maybe Laos. Maybe some shit in the Phillipines. Whatever it was those eyes were death. This was a businessman and this was the professional Johnny was looking for to begin with. Johnny needed work. He'd thought he would have to do some low grade shit for some useless drug dealers to begin with and work his way up with the Hells Angels or some garbage like that. But he'd got lucky, again. He noted to himself that luck had always run with him. How lucky he'd been to get across the border. How lucky to stop here at this strip club where there were hundreds of other bars in this city of Vancouver that he knew nothing about. Here, at this table, a life preserver.

And the eyes looking across at him saw all this on his face and twinkled. Business was good and getting better.

"I need you in Nanaimo." English with a heavy Asian accent. "Your Honda has been moved." Keys followed the photograph to the table. And then another photograph of a young kid sitting behind a white car sat upon both. "Eliminate." A long pause as it measured Johnny's response. "The money is under the passenger seat. I will have more work for you. I will be in touch."

And then the black haired trench-coated angels walked towards the red exit sign and vanished into what appeared to be mid-day sunshine that momentarily sliced the smoke and splattered the tables and closed. Johnny grabbed the keys and photos, headed to the bathroom to clean up and shave, dropped $200 on the bar, and walked into the sunshine.

So Johnny Hollywood got in that car and headed directly onto Georgia which turned into the Stanley Park Causeway and onto the three lane green spiked Lions Gate Bridge up onto Taylor Way and left on Highway 1 to the B.C. Ferry terminal. Johnny

wasn't sitting at that booth for two days
without dissecting an escape plan. Know your
territory. Know your routes in and out of the
city like the back of your hand. Stupid people
sat on their asses and drank beer and got
caught. They got lazy and stupid. Johnny
wasn't stupid. And so that ferry headed over to
the asshole of the world, Nanaimo. A place that
horseshoed to nowhere. It bounced people
either north or south and never west. Old farts
came to die in public paid housing and public
paid ambulances and public paid hospitals but
no one really stayed. First it was a coal mining
town with shacks to fit. A China town that
burned to the ground over 100 years ago.
Farmland, acres and acres of farmland, that
was turned into miner and banker shacks and
somewhat developed but mostly left to die
when the lumber mill closed. No mining, no
forestry, no fishery, some malls, some people
come to die, some realtors humping their way
to success, a city council merry with conference
centres that were permanently vacant and
bleeding. And a booming crack addiction,
small time prostitution rings, a circle of petty
crimes like maggots feeding upon each other as
in a Chinese maggot box. Some tourism, some
drugs coming in and out of the docks with the
hands that feed taking their cuts and

distributing to the addicted and the health professionals paying their mortgages on the miseries and teachers teaching the doomed offspring. Abandon hope all ye that enter, Dante's Inferno, Nanaimo.

And circling the streets endlessly at night was Joey in his little white Honda two door civic or prelude or some shit. The hood had been repainted black… by hand with a can or aerosol. Still with a pack of smokes on the dash and one in his lips and the car full of his peeps Joey was a big fucking deal. He wasn't good at school, his dad had made sure of that with the blood lessons in the alley. He glanced up at the rearview mirror and admired the scars across his eyebrows and lips. Made him look sexy. Chicks dug it. And he was tough as nails after all those whippings. Sure, he didn't win many fights but no one challenged him after a couple of bloody losses. Those riding with baby Joey were riding with the man. And when Joey found out that the small market he'd cut up of his friends and associates and his dad's buds was being cut into that by that little faggot nigger spook with those fucking dreads and his little two-timing slut bitch he had saddled up and went a looking for his competition. Nature abhors a vacuum. No guns. Baseball bats, knives, and an overloaded white something swerving and squealing its way around the old streets of Harewood.

The cell phone rang.

"Where?" little Joey couldn't believe it.

"At his house?" A pause.

"I'm on it."

Fucker was at his dad's house. The balls on that sack of shit. And he squealed his way back home, or what used to be, before they locked dad up, and the scum were still squatted there while the banks waited for a foreclosure.

And just about that time Keith had the old green minivan circling the neighbourhood looking for that rat's ass brother of his to make sure he understood he was in way over his head and that his market and his clients where his market and his clients. Jail or no jail you don't fuck a man like that. Especially not brother, not blood. Keith loved little Joey. Poor kid had taken most of the old man's worse drunken beat downs. A lot of times Keith had been out hustling for food money or beer for the old man and when he'd left it was all cool and when he'd got back Joey was always bleeding and his dad peering through his inch thick glasses rubbing his bald head and confused about what the hell he was doing in the alley with the police sirens coming again and his son bleeding at his feet. Two stupid bastards, thought Keith. It was hard to do business with those two dirtbags screwing it up all the time. And Keith was pretty sure that little Joey was going to screw up the business. Fuck, he'd screw up the Lord's Prayer if he knew the words. Joey always drew too much attention to himself. Always put the spotlight on himself with the latest clothes and a too fast car and hanging with peeps with mouths that ran on and on at the first sign of trouble. Little shit was probably trying to handle a problem with a baseball bat right now instead of using his brain and getting out some cash and buying out the competition. There's was no way this goof was going to make the Hell's Angels always drawing attention to himself. And now Keith was out and free and already cleaning up his mess again. He'd learned nothing from hanging out with his older brother. He didn't hate Joey. Loved the little guy. Blood was blood. He would rough him up a little then explain, again, how to run a drug business properly without drawing needless attention. Nothing loud and proud. Silent. Always good business. Always deliver. Always say thank you when you took the money. Never judge. Business was business and nothing more. Move on and get yours.

Little Joey's car hummed at 110 kph in the 50 kph streets as he zipped through Hamilton and Colliery and 5th Street and Howard. When he crossed 5th street and didn't stop at the sign his car bottomed out trailing 50 feet of sparks behind his car, the muffler roaring off somewhere down into a ditch. The boys in the back seat screamed like little sissies. A little driving and they wet themselves. Joey was smiling from ear to ear. He'd find that fucker and beat him to an inch of his life. He didn't notice all the lights on in the houses he was flickering past. First into second into third into fourth, brakes, hard left, hard right, second into first into second into third maybe fourth, brakes, hard left, hard right and again.

"Find him!" he screamed through his cocaine induced courage.

"Find him!"

"Find him!"

"Find him!"

Johnny Hollywood blankly took a left off the ferry and through the deserted downtown and abandoned buildings and brick laced warehouses. He knew this part of town without knowing it. The overgrown grass. The litter in the gutters. Suggestions of prostitutions in the 7-11s with their protection outside jittery from the crack and the plastic on the windows and the spray paint on the fence. He assumed the city workers would have been to the right off the ferry. Left was home. And a new beginning for Johnny Hollywood. A quick drive around and a look-see. A stop at one of these 7-11s and a smoke in the parking lot and he'd be on his way. The kid would be here. This was business town. And business looked good.

Keith saw the dumb fuck streaking across 5th Street and prodded the green minivan into action. Judging by the sparks Joey was in trouble and Joey was high and Joey was looking for trouble and Joey was going to end up dead or in jail and Joey couldn't handle either one so Keith prodded that minivan as quickly as it could go to catch that white prelude or civic or whatever piece of shit it was.

And as Johnny left the 7-11 he heard the metal on pavement and the sound of a muffler coming off a car, or rather that in reverse, and he put the cigarette in his mouth and slowly walked to his car and sat down and started the car and put his hand into the glove compartment and found the cold piece of steel he knew was there. A quick glance confirmed it was cleaned and loaded and ready for business. There must have been a lot of sparks from that idiot. Johnny knew it was him. He was lucky that way. Instinct told him it was a kid looking for trouble, teenagers screwing something up. Way too much noise, way too much attention. The cops might be bought but not all the citizens were, not yet. He rolled the silencer on the muzzle and put it on the seat beside him and moved towards the sound, south, back towards the water. What a Saturday night. What a fortunate event, he thought to himself. I'm fucking good. And he thought about putting that silencer under the kid's neck and pulling the trigger, stripping in the car, dumping the clothes off a bridge with the body, changing, and slowly, carefully, driving south to Victoria or north to Comox to the ferry system to get back to Vancouver and out of this shithole, mission accomplished. He knew he had approximately 12 hours to get back to Vancouver or he'd have to wait at least a month before trying the ferry system. That meant a month holed up in some crappy cheap motel watching bad Oprah reruns. Victoria sounded good. Rain started to bleed down into the mining town and the clouds moved in. Wind started to sweep down from the tiny mountains behind. Johnny smiled. Not much rain in California. Three days into his new country and the rain and clouds and small town attitude was suiting him. Darkness, rain, wind, what more could a man on a mission want? Could it get any easier?

JJ performed a snap U-turn in front of the old man's house with the sparks still flying out from under JJ's white piece of overloaded crap. One of his backseat riders smacked his head against the shoulder of his riding buddy and was knocked out immediately. The other one dazed himself against the window and cut his tongue. The front rider had been holding the "oh shit" handle with his window open to the rain so that when JJ performed the maneuver his door flew open and he was momentarily outside the car before he snapped back to the car and fell under the back tire where he then smacked his head on the wet asphalt and was knocked out cold.

As it happened the little nigger was actually outside the old man's house in the alley with his bitch dropping off some crack to a hand protruding from the downstairs bathroom window holding cash. He saw the white car slip past and snap and the ejection of a passenger before he grabbed the cash, slapped the plastic bag in the hand, grabbed his bitch, and quickly walked down the alley to Hamilton Street before breaking into a flat out run.

A green minivan whipped down
Hamilton about a hundred feet in front of the
nigger and bitch and was gone. They kept
going.

Keith thought JJ, the dumbass, would go
back to his old man's place, and try to get cash
from the scum that were squatting there. Keith
knew that only low-levels would do business
there at this point. There was no money. If
there was money it would take minutes
sometimes an hour to produce which meant
having to stay there and wait. You'd need to be
desperate to make a score to be there. Police
knew about the flop house at this point. There
was no disguising it as a college party house.
There was no bad tenant lie that could be
passed that could cover all the cars coming and
going. And at that point the hookers would be
showing up, sometimes with Johns, sometimes
without, with their track marks showing, and
their hair askew so that everyone knew their
business. At this point the crack house would
be bad. And if you showed up your licence
plate and car and description were going to get
made by the neighbours or the cops watching
the house. This was bad. JJ was so stupid
sometimes. Part of Keith wanted to leave the
little bastard at the crack shack to get busted
and get a taste of prison. But the other part of

him said this was family. It was his little man. True, one that had fucked him over for a piece of his action without telling him. But part of him hoped that JJ was going to come clean when he saw him. Maybe he got caught up in the excitement and forgot about coming to see him at Brannen Lake. He slowed down off Hamilton, pulled a right at the top of the hill, and came back down the hill.

And at 2 am Keith looked down upon his little brother JJ running down the street towards the alley beside a white piece of shit with some guy laying on the pavement and another guy trying to get out of the opened door.

Quickly Keith gunned the minivan down the hill, pulled left past the pavement pal, then right past the piece of shit, and turned a hard right in front of his brother and opened the door and stepped out and punched JJ hard in the stomach and held him as he fell under the streetlight which suddenly went out in one fluid motion.

The street wasn't lit well to begin with and the entire street was dark except the odd house window and the two car's headlights which quickly turned to one when Keith reached back in and moved his car off the road and turned it off.

At that time the dazed and bleeding occupant of JJ came to Keith with baseball bat in hand.

"Keith?"

"Yeah."

Keith reached down and pulled little JJ up to his knees then upright.

Keith looked to the baseball bat holder.

"Get that car off the road, turn it off, kill the lights, and pick up that meat off the pavement."

It ran back to the car and the lights went off.

"Joey, Joey, Joey."

JJ looked up at his older brother and fell towards him crying.

"I'm sorry. I'm sorry," gurgling out of his mouth.

Keith could see he was high. Probably they all were. Stupid, stupid, stupid.

JJ leaned over and vomited beside the minivan and his brother's shoes.

He was breathing hard either from the drugs or the punch.

And that's when Keith saw two blinding lights circle his eyes and felt the pain and saw the pavement coming up to his face and tasted the road dirt in his mouth.

Johnny parked the car.

Beautiful, he smiled too himself.

Some big guy had stopped his man.

Darkness surrounded his car as he pulled the lights off and turned the key off and rolled to a stop a house down from the minivan.

Blinking the rain out of his eyes he walked to three men. The baseball bat was going to be an issue. But just then it turned around and left back to the car. The lights went off and the guy went walking back to a man moaning on the road. Johnny kept moving forward and pulled his hoodie over his head and the gun from out of his jacket. His target was there, no question. Johnny had memorized that face on the ferry ride for 2 hours. He knew every inch of the shaved head and little neck and scarred face with one in particular over his right eye. The scars matched; no question. He pulled the butt end clear and smacked the big guy in the back of the head and he dropped like a sack of shit. He walked the extra three feet to the vomiting man and flicked the gun around in his palm and brought the muzzle up under the little fella's chin and squeezed the trigger.

An orange flash and JJ fell beside the driver's side front tire and Johnny looked down upon the big guy to see what was what.

Keith knew he was dead.

He knew the gun was expensive.

Groggily he staggered to his feet and put his left hand on the killer's shoulder for bracing. The brace held and grabbed his arm to steady him.

Keith saw the face and the blue eyes, the steady blue eyes, and nodded his head in understanding. He reached down for the body and the killer opened the sliding door and helped lift the body in and close it.

The killer grabbed two cigarettes, put them in his mouth, lit them and passed one to Keith.

Keith inhaled deeply.

"I've got this."

Johnny nodded and walked quickly and quietly to the car, started it, and slowly and quietly moved to 5th Street and headed West to the highway.

Keith got to the minivan, started it, and quietly drove off West to the highway. The Cowichan River is a much deeper and faster river than the Nanaimo River.

## Chapter 4

Joe's dad was a butcher. A hard working butcher who had no time for children but made them anyways. He was a practical no-nonsense human being. And so was his wife. They co-signed on their son's first house. Then they used the collateral to buy a second house. Then a third. Then an apartment building. Then some more. After a few years of experimenting they found the best way to make money in this game was to rent houses in tough areas of town to particular people. People that made their money on growing illegal substances. Whether it was making methamphetamines, crack cocaine or marijuana growing operations, the business rule was the same. I know what's going on, give me a cut, you proceed full speed ahead. The rent was a mere pittance compared to the cut they took in the drug business. They developed a reputation as a safe landlord. They weren't part of organized crime but they knew a few people.

And so when the rental beside Joe's house came available and some Vietnamese men phoned and met about the house they took it as is, old rotten carpets, moldy walls, fogged windows and all. They paid six months rent in cash up front. And then Joe's parents popped into see their cracked out son and encouraged him to kick the habit and kissed him on the head and left back to Vancouver. "No," they hadn't seen his wife, Rita-Joe, in several months but they would be sure to call him if they did. Her name was on the deed for Joe's house that the bank was foreclosing on, and once it came to that, Joe's parents would simply assume the mortgage and evict their son, renovate, and either sell or rent depending on how bad the neighbourhood felt and how much they could get for the place. They would tell Joe, of course, that it was out of their hands. The ferry ride back to Vancouver was unassuming and benign in their pale blue Cadillac.

And so it was convenient that when the Vietnamese got the grow operation running that Joe could meander through the fence and field of the overgrown lawn and simply request some pot and some crack.

"Why the fuck is he here?" Jason, the chemist of the crew, said.

"I guess his parents own the place or some shit."

Jason raised his eyebrows and got back to business.

Mixing crystal meth was a dangerous procedure, especially with so many pot plants mixing under the heat of the dangling grow light bulbs. They had the place wired beyond belief. Jason chuckled. Fucking death trap. It made it especially difficult to brew in this heat and moisture and with a crack head showing up two or three times per day and his sons banging on their door asking for some weed to sell, it made it very dangerous.

"We're going to have to get rid of these addicts you know," Jason mumbled.

"Mmm hmmm," his buddy mumbled back while intensely watering some plants.

"When that other place forecloses we're going to have these assholes flopping here."

"How long?"

"A few months. I figure six maybe."

"We got time."

This place was water, electricity, cover. That was all.

Six months and six figures, as long as they delivered good strong crystal and good strong plants.

Six months and then a new location. Keep on moving on.

As long as no one fucked up.

But then it fucked up.

A knock on the door at 1am.

A native woman, nice tits, nice long legs and a pretty tight ass for a woman in her late thirties. Teeth were still shiny white, not a lot of track marks. And unfortunately Jason was horny.

"Rita Joe," she said looking directly at Jason and bending over so he could see right down her shirt while she removed her shoes at the entrance and then she turned to put her shoes neatly by the door and bent over further letting Jason have a nice long look at that lovely ass. The face wasn't much but after three months of brewing chemicals and watering plants without leaving for so much as a Big Mac, Jason didn't care. Rita Joe looked like she could suck a golf ball through a water hose and Jason stared at her tits anyways.

Rita Joe could see him staring at her tits and bent over for him. She was desperate for her fix and he was kind of cute anyways. She just needed a couple of weeks of crystal to get her head straight and somewhere safe she could stay at for awhile before she would dry out and clean up. Rita Joe was broke and worse owed money. Worse she was married to Joe who was losing their house and losing everything they had to pay the debt back and Joe had let every crack addict in Nanaimo flop at their house so she didn't give a fuck anymore.

Jason grabbed her by her hips and pulled her to his throbbing member and started to rub it up and down on her. She didn't pull away but pushed back. Then she straightened and turned around and put her arms around his neck.

And so the arrangement was consummated in the moldy room on the mattress on the ground. Jason kept clean sheets and vacuumed a lot. That was one thing he couldn't stand – a dirty room. And when the drug cooker was finished he put his pants back on and got her a gram of crack and a spoon and a lighter and a syringe. And since he knew that the inventory was going to have to be accounted for he told his friend about upstairs on the mattress and his friend went upstairs and grabbed some relief for himself as well.

Rita Joe was happy with the room and the arrangement. Both were very respectful and clean and nice smelling. Both wore rubbers without any problems. And they both really really needed it and since she had a name on a mortgage with Joe's parents and they owned this place she figured she owned it too and so as far as she was concerned she was just taking care of a business partner by making sure the workers were satisfied. But mostly it gave Rita Joe time to think. She realized that if she stayed with Joe she would soon be out on the street with him and so she had to divorce. That wasn't an issue. Joe beat her so much that she had moved past the battered wife and into the killing wife phase. She would be very happy when he died with a syringe in his arm and that stupid shit eating grin on his face that he got through those coke bottle glasses and half shaved beard and fall off his face comb over when he got his high. She showered and shot up and got some clothes out of the only piece of luggage she had brought with her and ran them through the washer and dryer. She was leaning over the washing machine in her underwear when she felt hands go up her shirt and start squeezing her breasts and knew it was Jason when she was pressed in to the washer by his throbbing cock. The other guy always needed some help and coaxing. Not Jason. She smiled. Maybe this was her way out.

The problem with the grow op is that the pot lights were blowing the 15amp fuses hourly. No matter how that guy configured the extension chords and staggered the lamp sequences they kept blowing the fuse. And it was becoming a pain in the ass.

"Jason are you finished?"

No answer. He knocked again.

"Jason?"

He was pretty sure they were finished the steady squeaking of the mattress had stopped a minute ago.

"Yeah. Ok so we need to bypass the meter."

"Damn. That's what I figured too."

This was a problem. Generally you could run a 150 plant grow-op in an empty house as long as you didn't ever run the stove and barely ran the washing machine and dryer. Bypassing the hydro meter was a bit risky. Most of the hydro meter readers were bought men but some weren't. No one was going to say anything about a doubling of the meter consumption or even tripling of the house's consumption. The computer would flag it only if their power consumption dropped off the grid. Some eager beaver back at Hydro's main office in Vancouver was going to flag the drop off as a bypass. However, that could take four to six months. They only needed three months left. So far the crack heads had been kept to a minimum. It was mainly Joe's sons and Joe himself that were making daily or weekly treks through the backyard. And so far they had escaped any police attention. If they didn't deliver the pot on time it was bad news. Someone somewhere was going to figure they had been skimming and then a collector was going to be sent and that meant those two were going on a direct trip to a pig farm in Coquitlam. Jason had been through this more than a couple of times. He had earned his reputation as someone who could deliver. The problem with this house was that it was the first time they had rented a house that 100amp service. They had thought the house was 200 amp service and thought it was a lot newer than it was. And someone had played with the wiring and then dry walled over it and they couldn't get the sequence right that wouldn't blow a 15amp circuit every hour. They were losing time and losing sleep and that meant getting sloppy. And that meant a failed delivery.

"I know someone," Rita Joe said.

"Joe has an electrician flopped out at his place."

Jason considered that for a moment.

If this crack head electrician bypassed the meter then they had three months and everything was fine except they owed Rita Joe and the electrician and if Joe was there and knew about it then Joe and then probably everyone at the crack house.

That was a lot of debtors. That was a lot of people coming to the door and saying, hey, I heard something, hint, hint, hint.

Not that the stupid junky was going to phone the police because the supply was going to get cut off then where were they going to go and they knew what organization Jason and his friend worked for. But still they would want their crack and crystal meth cheap. That they probably could do. But no pot. The pot couldn't be touched. And no attention to the house.

They could call in for help but the Red Scorpions weren't someone you just called in to provide a little muscle. If they made the call then someone would answer and someone would die and then the police would be here and the grow op was over. They had to keep the house quiet and the plants growing.

Jason kneeled beside Rita Joe and held her hand.

"Yes. Please go get him."

Rita Joe really liked him. He was always gentle and he held her hand and he smelled nice and though he was maybe 15 years younger than her she could still bring children for him. She wanted children again and a husband who would treat them nice. Jason would treat them nice. She could tell. His sparkly eyes. The way he held her and came and breathed into her ear.

She squeezed his hand back and then got up and showered and dressed and went through the backyard to Joe's place. There was a path permanently cut through the two foot grass from Joe's parents place to Joe's place. Fully grown evergreens hid the backyard and the abandoned tent trailer and two trucks. Little Joey's first truck that Joe had bought him that had died about two months after he got it and Joe promised to fix it but never did. The moonlight lit her way through the backyard and to the hole in the fence that she found and gently nudged her way through the self-made gate and walked over to Joe's and into the basement.

The place stank of garbage. Four people were passed out in the living room and none of them were Joe or the electrician. There was a prostitute who she knew but couldn't remember her name and her pimp, big Bubba. And a couple of guys that might have been strangers and probably were and bottles of whiskey and scotch and rum and beer cans dumped everywhere. Fuck, she thought to herself. Even if they get Joe out of here there's no way this place is going to be worth anything. She wasn't going to get a dime out of this and she was going to owe the Hell's Angels a lot of money for the crack and a little bit for the heroin that she'd been dabbling a bit in. There was no sign of Keith or JJ, little Joey. She had hoped little Joey was going to be something and she felt he was going to make it. He had such a smile. She gently opened the door to his bedroom and found the electrician passed out on the soiled bed in what looked like a grey t-shirt and black underwear that were exposing half of his ass and blue jeans that were exposing half of his underwear and his knees were on the floor and the mattress corner between his crotch and his arms flailed out on either side of his head like he was trying to make a snow angel like Keith and JJ used to make in the alley beside the house while she drank beers and laughed and laughed and there was a white bandage tied around his left finger.

She put her hand on his back and felt that he was still breathing and he stirred. He moaned and smell of whiskey wafted upwards with it.

"Rita Joe?"

"Hi," she smiled back in the darkness.

"Hey," he said and pushed his way and turned so that he was sitting on the edge of the mattress.

He could see Rita Joe with her hair all done up nicely smiling at him in the street light that came through front window and through the front room and down the hallway and into the room.

"What's up?"

"Shhhhhhh," she whispered and held his hand and squeezed it.

Damn, he thought. She wasn't the best looking woman in the world but she sure had nice tits and a nice ass and it had been a long time since he been with a woman. He sat there then thinking about the last time he had been with a woman. Then he sat there looking for a bottle of something that had replaced the woman.

"Hey, do you think you could bypass a meter for me?"

"Hydro meter?" he whispered back. "Yeah, yeah. No problem. Can you help me find something to drink. I'm pretty thirsty. Then I got to piss. Where's the meter?"

Rita Joe found started grabbing bottles and shaking them and found one that sounded half full and gave it to him.

He took a swig.

"Thanks," he smiled back. "Hey are you getting back with Joe? You two should get back together," he whispered and smiled at her hoping the answer was no so that maybe just maybe he could take her to the bathroom with him.

"No," she smiled back.

He felt something twitch.

"I've got to go, just a second, let me wash my face then I'll come with you. Where's the meter?"

"Next door," said Rita Joe.

That didn't surprise him. He knew that's where most of the pot and crack that they were getting was coming from. It was a pretty nice setup. Grow it over there and sell it here. Here, Joe's house, had good lane access. Three ways to get to the house. Three ways to disperse the traffic. That was good. And Joe had let him stay here for awhile while he sobered up and found another job after getting fired from the mill when the mill "restructured".

He stumbled his way to the bathroom and fought the gag reflex from the pee smell and found the toilet, not that it mattered since most missed, and pissed and flushed. Then he splashed some water on his face and hair and ran his hair through it and made it so that it resisted standing up on the back of his head. Then he put his head under the faucet and drank some water for fresh breath. There was no soap but he ran his hands under the water rubbing them back and forth for at least a minute feeling the water and trying to find a better mental place than what he was in. When he found that the water he drank made him a little steadier he drank some more. Then he zipped his fly up and pulled his blue jeans up and tucked his shirt in and put some more water in his hair and ran his fingers through his hair some more. Rita Joe had a really nice ass. He hoped he might get a look at it.

"Ok," he said to her when he got out of the bathroom.

He couldn't find her right away but when his head stopped spinning he saw her staring in at Joe's room. He walked down to her and looked in the doorway. Joe was passed out naked on the mattress. The sheets must have fallen off and exposed him.

Rita Joe was going to miss that cock. When Joe was right he was really something. But he wasn't right anymore and she closed the door and smiled at the electrician who had tried to comb his hair and had spilled water all over the front of his t-shirt and shoulders doing so. She put a hand on his arm and guided him outside.

They walked back to the broken fence and found the self-made gate and back to the house and back to Jason and his friend. Jason and his long straight black hair and strong chiseled jaw and pointy black eyes and warm smile. He was normal and she needed normal and hoped she could keep him. The way he was glancing at her tits she felt she might just be able to keep normal. He was still interested, a lot interested, and that was something.

"Hi," she smiled at him.

"Hi," he smiled back.

Damned if she didn't do it.

His friend came to the window, holding the gun, and looked out at the electrician. He looked a mess.

"Shit Jason, I don't know. He looks like a burnout," he said in his thick Vietnamese accent. "A burnout. He fuck up, we fucked."

Jason had a good look at the electrician. He had clothes on that weren't washed for days and he had a white piece of cloth tied on his left hand index finger. He guessed that the finger had been cut off as a warning on a debt that he owed the organization.

"Rita Joe," Jason grabbed her hand and gently turned her face to him with his other hand. "This guy looks like someone who's been drunk for days."

"I know it. I have," the electrician said. He could see the disappointment in the guy holding Rita Joe's hand.

He held the left hand up with the blood soaked cloth. "Yeah, I think I've met your bosses," he breathed. "I owe them but I can help them and maybe you guys can put in a good word, eh?"

Jason looked at his friend and shrugged.

He shrugged back smiling.

Maybe this would work out after all. A bought man fixing their meter, fixing their electrical problems. Once the meter was bypassed they could put 30 amp fuses in for the 15 amps and keep the lamps the same way. The wires would get hot but Jason and his friend would work shift work through the final days of the grow op. They so much as sniffed a fire they would shut it down, grab the weed they had, and the meth and crack and hit the car. If they got just 60 days they'd be good. If they got 90 days they were fully made. But in two months they would have the plants fully grown and the bags of pot would start to fill the basement and they'd have enough so that when they showed up at the warehouse they'd be just fine. A couple hundred pounds light but that would be fine. Not all soil and not all seeds grew the same. It would be explainable.

"Yeah my friend. We will do that for you. Rita Joe says you are very good."

It wasn't that hard.

"You got tools?"

"Yup," Jason said and let go of Rita Joe's hand and went into the living room and got the carefully packed electrical tool boxes and brought them outside to the electrician who was already at the meter.

"I'll need some light," the electrician said.

Jason grabbed a flashlight out of the box and opened the boxes up for him and the electrician grabbed some goggles and put them on and some heavy leather gloves and a then he grabbed cutting pliers and snapped the wire holding the screw that held the meter clamp tight. The meter wire would have to be put back carefully so that it didn't look tampered and he had cut it just so that he could twist and tie it back together so that as long as someone didn't look too hard it would past a visual quick look. The meter readers looked at so many during a day anyways that by the time it was 4pm on a Thursday they could give a flying fuck what condition it was in, they were going home in 30 minutes and could careless. And hopefully it was a meter that was in the organization's back pocket anyways. Most were.

And then the grabbed a Phillips screw driver bit and put it on the drill and he unwound the Phillips screw that held the large metal clamp on the glass cased meter and he unwound it.

Then the shakes started a little bit to come into the electrician's hands. He was thinking about maybe getting a piece of Rita Joe's ass but now he was thinking that if he could quickly do this he might have his debt forgiven. And then he got to shaking a bit more and he started thinking mostly about getting another drink.

Jason wasn't really looking at the electrician's hands and didn't see them shake. He was looking at Rita Joe's blue jeaned covered ass in the flickering street light. The light was turning off for about 10 seconds at a time then it would come back on. Jason was thinking how good it was for his luck. If there was anybody peering at their bedroom windows at this house at this time in the morning all they would see is a bit of fog and rain and they would be distracted by the turning on and off the streetlight.

Rita Joe felt warm inside that Jason was looking so hard at her ass. It was nice to be wanted again the way Joe had used to want her in the beginning when first got their house and before the kids and before the drinking got to become a habit. Rita Joe determined to clean up and to put the pieces of her life together. She would offer to do it with Jason but if Jason didn't want to go clean with her that was fine. She was pretty sure that she could do it on her own now. She smiled back at Jason. He had been so good for her. And so she didn't see the electrician shaking.

His hands wouldn't stop shaking. Maybe he hadn't eaten anything in several days. He couldn't remember anything more than some packages of junk from 7-11 in those shaking hands. And some whiskey. And some slaps to the cheek from big Bubba. He couldn't remember why only that he had been knocked down and everyone had laughed and he'd found a bottle of something on the floor or had crawled to one and had either been kicked in the ass or pushed down but after everyone had started laughing he laughed too and the kicking had stopped.

The light kept turning off and on and that Jason guy kept moving the flashlight on him and so he was working mostly blind. When he pulled the glass meter straight back it almost hit in the nose. But it was off.

"Hey, keep the light on here eh?"

Jason put the flashlight back.

Whoops. For an older woman she had a real tight ass and it was hard not to look at it. But he kept looking at it.

The electrician put the glass meter in his left hand while he grabbed the 12 gauge wires. Not easy shit to work with. Not with shaking hands. All he had to do now was to disconnect the white wire from the copper jumper that went to the meter's neutral being careful not to touch the lay-in neutral connector that had the 240 volt load. It was a single phase. A three phase four wire was hard. This was old and it was easy. Except his hands were shaking and his eyes were glowing a bit red and he touched the load lead and the lead both at the same time with his right hand and the 100 amps welded his hand in place and the streetlights all down the street flickered and the power went out and the electrician was still shaking and twitching and burning.

Rita Joe screamed.

And Jason knew it was over.

And he and his buddy had brought pushed the electrician's body off of the meter with a wooden stick and grabbed its stiffness and brought it inside while Rita Joe sat there crying and shaking.

And though Jason slapped her and his friend slapped her they couldn't stop so they injected her with a lot of heroine so that she stopped moaning and bitching so that they could talk and think. Neither one could fix the meter and neither one wanted to after they saw the burned hand still left on the meter and parts of leather glove. The power had come back on later that morning all down the street. The hydro workers must have found the short and flicked the power back on but not in their house.

In their house with the $250,000 of equipment and chemicals and inventory that wasn't ready for market it was cold and dark and quiet.

Until two days later after they hadn't answered their cell phones or house phone that someone knocked. There was nowhere to run. A blue mini-van had pulled into the driveway and two older small men, former North Vietnamese Army men probably, collectors, showed up for Jason and his friend and a man known as Willi tagged along. Willi had wispy red hair and was balding and had a big hooked nose and dead dark brown eyes and a nasty reputation as a mutilator of prostitutes from the downtown eastside that he tortured and fed to his pigs on his Coquitlam farm just so that he could get his formulas of pain just right so that when the Hells Angels called upon him to talk to people like Jason and his friend as a favour to the Red Scorpions or for people like Rita Joe who failed to pay their debts, then Willi would have the formula just perfected.

Willi found Rita Joe on the mattress and kicked at her.

"Not yet," he said to her. "You're lucky that your parents have said they have a use for you. But we'll meet I'm guessing."

Rita Joe only remembered being pushed before passing out and then waking with police all around the house and being taken out of the house on a stretcher and being driven to the hospital in an ambulance. She never saw Jason again.

The police announced the seizure of 150 pot plants and at least $100,000 of grow operation equipment had been seized at a house that was known to police. The coroner had been called upon the discovery of a body in a bathtub. At least what was left of a body, if the rumours were correct. No one had been arrested however they had several suspects and were asking for the public's assistance. Joe's parents had to call in BC Hydro to fix an electrical problem before they could rent the house again.

## Chapter 5

Bubba left William Head medium security prison in Victoria and got in his Lincoln and headed north. Three years of an eight year prison sentence and another six months out on day passes and monthly parole hearings before he was finally let go on probation and a weekly check-in with a parole officer and a weekly check in with the RCMP office to give his location.

Some son-of-a-bitch was going to pay.

Those steely blue eyes headed directly north back to Nanaimo to reclaim his collection job and his territory and his place. He stopped at the Hells Angels clubhouse and was let in. He left with a thirty-eight special with serial numbers filed off and some rounds. That

Lincoln tore around the streets of Harewood looking and looking and looking.

That filthy bitch prostitute Janis lied about him and the other guy when he knew there was no other guy and she was going to die. He knew she'd be there. And he found that black nigger in an alley in the exact same house that he'd made his own after they had taken Joe down and he found that bitch too and some fucker claiming they were both his. Some guy they called the apple pimp.

The little nigger could work for him, he was profitable. And that little bitch whore would come around for him and start working for him again. But another man working them both, that shit had to end. And so he sat under the street light loading the rounds into the .38 Smith & Wesson Special. He basked in it's glow until he was good and proper fucked up with booze and pot and he drove that Lincoln two doors down to a place where he knew the three of them were holed up. And he kicked the door down.

Apple Pimp was a big man. Cut and tall you could see his ripped ab muscles under the white t-shirt he always wore. His dark curly hair cropped a masculine face and hazel eyes that were perfectly placed. He was quick and lean. And when Bubba burst into the house the nigger screamed. But he didn't. He ran directly at Bubba.

Bubba saw him coming got that .38 unreeled from his track pants quicker than the Apple Pimp thought possible and he pumped him full of four bullets as he slid down the stairs and landed at his feet in a heap. The little nigger flew out the back glass patio doors and jumped off the patio with a bag of weed in hand. He went running to the 7-11 to get his bitch before she got back and Bubba pumped her too with that red hot .38. And Bubba stormed around the house and found no one but the dead Apple Pimp bleeding upside down on the stairs. So he sheathed his gun and got back into the Lincoln under the street light and he noticed that a lot of the lights in the houses were on. He had left the front door open in his haste and the shots must have been heard. And when he turned the key on his old Lincoln nothing happened. He had left the lights on and all there was now was a "gggggrrr" "gggggrrr" and click click click click of a dead battery that was too old from waiting for him to finish with William Head. And so the police found him with a red hot pistol in that Lincoln and when they closed on him he put that gun in his mouth and ended big beautiful Bubba with a flash and a pop.

Michael Munro

## 6-6-o

Up in his cherry picker the BC Hydro worker was changing a light bulb that had been flickering off and on when a man came out of the house.

"Hey… How's it going? Do you think you could do something about that third six? It kind of creeps me out."

"Not really supposed to do that but … wait a second."

He looked underneath and sure enough there were three sixes.

He took a screw driver out of his front pocket and etched the top line off the last six.

"How's that?"

"That's good. Thank you."

Back at the office the Hydro workers were moving.

Old Damian Howard's desk was one of the last thing to move out of the old rally hall. It was a big oak desk. Howard had been here at this desk for probably 40 years doing paperwork. Assigning numbers to everything from telephone poles to houses to lights. He was retired 10 years now and no one used this hall much for more than storage of old records and old equipment that they needed occasionally for parts. The desk was stained dark. Probably worth a lot of money. When they pulled the drawers out a photograph fell out. A few in fact. Three soldiers in black in white. It looked like World War II maybe. One of them was tapping his penis on a dead German's soldier's bare ass and smiling at the camera. It was grotesque and disturbing and the workers thought it was probably fake. One of the guys moving the desk looked at it and laughed and crumpled it and threw it in the garbage can and got back to moving the old desk.

All of this was going to be sold.

## About the author

Michael Munro is a graduate of the 1992 Langara University (then known as Vancouver Community College, Langara Campus) Journalism program. He went on to study English Literature at British Columbia Open University (which is now known as Thompson River University).

Prior to that he made brief and somewhat lucid stops at Capilano College (now known as Capilano University) where he studied something including philosophy and Malaspina University (now known as Vancouver Island University) where he remembers a business course.

Somewhere between then and there he worked for some community newspapers in Vancouver and Nanaimo covering everything from the Vancouver Canucks (Pat Quinn era) to general beat and court reporting and the political scene having interviewed three British Columbia premiers and watched all three get booted out of office. Not due to any of his work but because this is British Columbia, home of the wild wild west. He was once fired from a newspaper for writing a column about leveling a neighbouring community and turning it into a golf course (story to come). He is currently and surprisingly employed.

Michael grew up on the Queen Charlotte Islands (now known as Haida Gwaii) and moved to North Vancouver Island then regressed in Vancouver and Nanaimo while his hair grayed. The community is currently considering changing its name.